A big thank you to my son Stefano
for his creativity, his vision
and especially, his patience.

Contact: rdidonato321@gmail.com

ISBN 979-8-648-03335-1

Giraffe Has a Bug

Written and Illustrated by
Robert DiDonato

One happy day a young giraffe
was drinking in the lake.
A bug was napping on a leaf
and did not want to wake.

Somehow that little tiny bug
who was so very near
rolled off the leaf, (and to its grief),
dropped in Giraffe's left ear.

The poor giraffe then squirmed around
and soon began to shout.
She tried the very best she could
but could not get it out.

Bunny, Beaver, Bird and Lion
noticed some commotion.
The bunny was the first to speak.

But though she tried some bunny hops,
the bug stayed put, you see.

The bug held on and didn't move.
It stayed just where it was.
And then to make it even worse
that bug began to buzz!

By now Giraffe was really sad
and asked the bird for help.
Birdie poked inside her ear
so hard she gave a Yelp!

He belted out a scary roar
so loud the trees did shake.
The bug went deep into her ear.
It was a big mistake!

Her
friends had thought that they had done
as much as they could do.
They
thought that they could help her out
but really had no clue.

Giraffe decided to ask big brother
to help her with a plan.
She asked if he could help her out.
Her brother said (I can.

Big brother gently whispered then
into his sister's ear.
Bunny, Beaver, Bird and Lion
all stretched their necks to hear.

And when they finally gave up hope
the bug just flew away.
The animals were so surprised they
shouted out

They wondered what it was he said.
How could she really know?
She smiled a clever smile and said

We just asked the bug to go.

ISBN 979-8-648-03335-1

Made in the USA
Monee, IL
01 June 2020